You Spoke Prose, I Heard Poetry is an intimate duet between narrative and verse—where story speaks, and poetry listens. Reena Kapoor's evocative prose grounds the reader in lived experience with clarity and restraint, each story a window into complex emotional worlds.

In response, Kate Adams's poems rise like an inner voice—resonant, intuitive, and brave—answering not with explanation, but with emotional truth. This is not a mirror, but a conversation. Together, Kapoor and Adams weave a rich tapestry of human feeling—where prose observes, poetry reveals, and silence is filled with meaning. A stunning exploration of connection, voice, and the spaces in between.

—**Geri Spieler, author of *Housewife Assassin: The Woman Who Tried to Kill President Ford.***

Open this gem at random. An evocative image draws you in. Read the engaging story; whimsical, touching, thought-provoking. Then the lyrical poem.

To be effective, a writer needs memory and imagination: Reena has both. Kate's sonnets add music to them. Reena's hundred-word prose vignettes are poignant; we glimpse distant lands and cultures. The flash-fiction stories explore a large canvas of themes and emotions.

Throughout history every art form has inspired other vehicles. Here the authors give us three windows, all equally beautiful. This book needs to be kept by one's bedside and savored often. A triple treat with sprinkles.

—**Harish Saluja, filmmaker, painter, writer, music producer and radio host.**

I0778636

The situations in this collection provide a conversation between the dimension of prose and the concision of poetry, expanding the reach of both with their own notable outcomes.

We read about a daughter who learns that a good marriage is about remarrying each day as her parents did, a girl who thinks she has cancer when her period starts, a woman who dies happy because she talked daily to a prank caller she believed was her lost son. The authors take ordinary circumstances and bring them to life through quirks the reader can easily relate to.

—Marianne Brems,
author of *Stepping Stones* and the chapbooks
***In Its Own Time, Unsung Offerings*, and *Sliver of Change*.**

You Spoke Prose, I Heard Poetry

A Duet

Stories by

Reena Kapoor

Poems by

Kate Adams

walnutpublication.com

INDIA • UK • USA

Copyright © Reena Kapoor & Kate Adams, 2025

All rights reserved. No part of this publication may be reproduced, stored in a retrieval system, or transmitted in any form or by any means, electronic, mechanical, recording or otherwise, without the prior written permission of the publisher or the author.

This is a work of fiction. Names, characters, places and incidents are either the author's imagination or are used fictitiously and any resemblance to any actual person living or dead, events and locales is entirely coincidental.

Paperback ISBN: 979-8-89171-231-7

Hardback ISBN: 979-8-89171-232-4

eBook ISBN: 979-8-89171-233-1

First Published in July, 2025

Published by Walnut Publication
(an imprint of Vyusta Platforms Private Limited)

www.walnutpublication.com

India

Unit# 909, 9th Floor, Wave Silver Tower, Sector-18, Noida - 201301

UK

71-75 Shelton Street, Covent Garden, London, WC2H 9JQ, UK

Distributed by

DEDICATIONS

For my parents,
eternally

RK

For my longtime companion,
a daughter of the Raj

KA

CONTENTS

THE STORYTELLER

THE POET

INTRODUCTIONS

INTRODUCTION TO THE PROSE

ALL STORIES IN THE WORLD ARE ABOUT LOVE

Two years ago, on a lark, I began writing one-hundred-word stories—exactly a hundred words, not more, nor less. Partly as a craft exercise, partly to see what might arrive within such constraints, to capture our condition. Unsurprisingly, the restraint forced an illuminating focus on essentials.

I began publishing these tiny tales online, on my Substack *Arrivals and Departures*. Some of them even became progenitors for longer ones.

One day my talented poet friend and co-author found them and asked if she could write sonnets inspired from (albeit not identical to) these tales. I immediately said, "Yes!"

And here we are!

—*Reena Kapoor*

INTRODUCTION TO THE POETRY

CONNECTIONS
CROSSING CONTINENTS

As my dedication indicates, I live with "a daughter of the Raj," a woman of European ancestry who grew up in India, living there until she was fifteen. Through her, I have expanded my purely American horizons all the way to Vijayawada, to Madras, to Calcutta, as she still speaks their names—even as those very horizons proved porous to the increasing presence of Indian culture in the distant purview of Silicon Valley. Those broadened horizons opened still further upon reading Reena's stories, inviting me to enter that world via my own favorite medium, poetry.

Just as I love to hear my companion's voice modulate back into the music of the Indian English she grew up with whenever she's in that milieu, so I like to think my own voice finds poetic music in response to Reena's grounded, even gritty, tales, in American English, of daily life on the subcontinent. This book evidences the richness of that meeting of East and West, however complicated—even now, in its twenty-first century diaspora.

—*Kate Adams*

HOW TO READ THIS BOOK

This is a book of micro stories by Reena; this is a book of poems by Kate.

Each chapter of the book combines a micro story, with a poem inspired by the story, along with a work of photo-art by Reena to emphasize the mood.

Each chapter is meant to create and encompass a world within. Unlike most books, this one is meant to be consumed accordingly—not all in one go, but in little nuggets, one chapter, one enclosed world at a time.

So, here's what we suggest . . .

Sit down, take a deep breath, get familiar with the introductions and preambles. Then pick a chapter, any chapter and dive in. Read the chapter's double-title and take in the accompanying photo-art; let that have its way with you.

Then read the micro story. Read it out loud. Given the story's brevity, give every word your full attention. Let it surprise you, puzzle you, perhaps entertain you, and, we hope, move you. Just sit with whatever it brings.

Then move on to the poems, usually a sonnet. Read that out loud and let it sink it. The poem is meant to carry echoes of—although not exactly reflect—the micro story. See if you can hear that and give the poetry its due.

We suggest you take in no more than one, maybe two, or, maximum, three stories in a sitting. Let each of them leave you with something to feel, ponder, intuit the world through. Come back to the book to gather more of these tales, when and as the mood strikes, or interest nudges you.

This format, this combination, this whole compilation is an experiment; we would love to hear from you what worked, what you wish it was more or less of—or wasn't.

With love,
Kate & Reena

FOR THE LIVING /
RUDALI SONG

For The Living

Northwest Frontier Province, Undivided India
1946

In 1946, my grandmother became a young widow. Her husband fell from a rooftop and died.

Their son, my uncle, who witnessed the incident, went into deep shock.

Per tradition in northwestern India at the time, *rudalis* arrived at the house to mourn. *Rudalis* were professional women mourners whose job was to help those grieving, embody, experience and process their grief. They did this by weeping openly, helping the family do the same.

My grandmother shocked everyone by defying tradition. She turned the women away.

When questioned, she said, "I must attend to my son's suffering first. I'll mourn later."

RUDALI SONG

Northwest Frontier Province, Undivided India
1946

He clambers to the roof, retrieves the ball,
cursing as he climbs. His second son
so thoughtless yet again, playing, running,
bouncing in the courtyard where high walls

can hem him in. The father looks down, calls.
And suddenly, the roof gives way, he's falling,
fallen, broken on the ground, the ones
left living stupefied, the boy undone . . .

Rudalis come to help the widow weep
and wail, to raise grief in her body, shake
it out. Dry-eyed, voice clear, she turns them all

away. "No, not for me, your high rudali
song. My son, he needs me first, to keep
the shock at bay. My mourning, it can wait." ❖

2

THE CHAI-WALLAH'S DEBT / TENFOLD

THE CHAI-WALLAH'S DEBT

Chai-wallah, a tea vendor

On the train to his ailing mother, Shri sipped his chai. Suddenly the train started moving. The *chai-wallah* outside yelled, "Two rupees!"

Inside, Shri fought to free his gnarly wallet from a loose pocket seam. He ripped out a note, throwing it out of the window. The chai-wallah caught it. Just then they both realized it was two thousand rupees! Shri slapped his forehead.

Cursing, he reached his mother's village—too late. People at her door were reminiscing about her prescient wisdom. She left him a letter that began, "Son, give without regret. The universe returns tenfold . . ." and twenty thousand rupees.

TENFOLD

Shri sips his chai. The old chai-wallah cries,
"Two rupees!" as the train begins to move.
Shri fishes for his wallet, tries to choose
a note and pass it back in time. It flies

from hand to hand, just as he realizes
it's two thousand rupees, not just two.
He smacks his forehead: *Hai Ram*! What a fool!
And worse than that, he's late: his mother dies

before he makes it home. Days later, lifts
the envelope she's left him, opens it.
"My son, I hope by now you understand

one thing: what you put in another's hand
comes back to you tenfold. Now you're a man,
here's twenty thousand rupees, parting gift." ❖

3

Denial /
Weighted Down

DENIAL

Daughters meant dowry and debt. Most parents prayed for sons.

Scientific advancements arrived. Doctors could see in the womb, determine the gender of the baby and abort female fetuses. The villagers were jubilant.

With an overpopulation of young men, the village became unsafe for the few remaining girls. Many daughters-only families left for the city. There the daughters discovered they could study more.

When the village boys came of age, there weren't enough women to marry. They contacted the city families. Those girls refused. The boys—now men—weren't sufficiently educated.

The village elders decided educating girls must be prohibited.

WEIGHTED DOWN

Daughters, they meant dowries, they meant debt;
most parents prayed for sons. When science came,
few female fetuses survived, remained
to match the males; and soon the girls all left

the village with its swarming boys. They claimed
an education in the city, leapt
beyond the boys they'd left behind. Bereft
of brides, old village life broke down, old ways

rejected by the young. Those women who
had run the gauntlet, somehow made it through,
refused to sacrifice their bodies, lives.

Slowly they could see it, how they'd bowed
before, weighted down by debt and dowries.
Now—*Don't educate the girls!* the elders cry.

4

FAIR TREATMENT / RELIEF

Fair Treatment

Jury selection was almost done. Several potentials had been thanked and excused, for admitting to not being able to "put [their] biases aside." The rest of us unwashed masses watched tensely from the not-yet-called pool.

The petite public prosecutor addressed final juror number twelve. "You'd mentioned your father was arrested in the '80s, correct?"

"Yes ma'am," he nodded.

She didn't blink. "So, do you think he was treated fairly by the justice system?"

Just say yes and be done, please!

"Yeah, he was treated fairly by the justice system." He hesitated. "But not by my mother!"

The courtroom erupted in laughter.

RELIEF

Hot and sweaty in the airless room,
I watch the young D.A. interrogate
the final jurors, wishing that the wait
would end. These legal types seem to assume

that everyone is biased, heading straight
for prejudice. So by late afternoon,
I'm desperate for relief. Fresh face. "Now, you've
revealed your father was arrested, jailed.

So, was he treated fairly by the law?"
Oh, please, say yes, and then we can be done.
A tension penetrates the air and runs

around the room. That face becomes becalmed,
ship on a sea of memory. "The law was fair."
We laugh as he declares, "But not my mom!" ❖

5

LOOK INSIDE /
THE MEASURE OF THE MAN

LOOK INSIDE

Raju happily married off his daughter Shaili. He missed her dearly. Shaili seemed happy at first but within months became forlorn. One day when she visited him, Raju noticed bruises on her arms.

Against everyone's advice, Raju confronted Shaili's husband.

The husband scoffed. "And so? You should have disciplined her better growing up!"

Raju said, "I smacked Shaili once. She was five. An old woman who witnessed it, berated me. I never did it again."

"What did the woman say?"

"She asked me what weakness made me resort to violence? Or was I just too stupid to communicate with words?"

The Measure Of The Man

Raju's daughter Shaili, freshly married,
starts out happy, then soon seems—forlorn.
She comes to visit him; he sees she carries
bruises on her arms. Against friends' warnings,

he confronts the husband, who just stares
him down: "You didn't discipline her very
well!" "I smacked her once, and got the scorn
of one who witnessed it, left me so torn

I never did again." "What did they tell
you?" Raju takes the measure of the man—
or rather, of himself. Hopes he has heard

the truth enough to speak it now. "What well
of violence just surfaced in your hand,
too stupid to communicate with words?'" ❖

6

CULTIVATED DARKNESS / WITH A TWIST

CULTIVATED DARKNESS

Simple, obedient Sana, charged with murdering her parents, wouldn't defend herself. The village shunned her.

Sana's aunt, who'd left the village in disgrace decades ago, arrived. Speaking in Sana's defense, she revealed Sana had three college-educated brothers, and two high-school educated, married sisters. But her parents didn't educate Sana, even rejected the humblest marriage offers. They kept Sana an illiterate dependent, focused on taking care of them.

Long ago the aunt had suffered similarly and run away from her home and village.

The judge awarded Sana a ten-year sentence—and most of her parents' estate for education and for living independently.

With A Twist

Charged with murdering her parents, she
refuses to defend herself, stays mute.
No one gets it. No one can refute
the evidence. It's all a mystery.

Simple Sana, youngest child, cutest
of them all—the villagers don't see
how it was her. They struggle to believe.
No one ever saw signs of abuse . . .

Exiled aunt comes back to testify.
"Sana's brothers? Educated. Sisters,
too. But her? Illiterate, to wait

on mom and dad; all suitors soon denied."
Her sentence? Yes, ten years, but with a twist:
the full inheritance of the estate.   ❖

7

LANDLINE CONNECTIONS /
AT LAST

LANDLINE CONNECTIONS

Bored, Talli and his friends made prank phone calls to strangers. One evening an old lady lovingly answered, "Son! I've been waiting. . ."

Talli ended the call. Oddly, he called her back. She continued, "Son, I miss you so much. . ."

Soon Talli was calling the lady daily. And listening to her lovingly recount happier days.

One day she didn't answer. A week went by. Talli tracked her number to an empty "For Sale" house.

The neighbors said, "She passed away peacefully, believing her wastrel son called everyday."

Talli asked, "Where's her son?"

They shook their heads. "He died ten years ago."

At Last

Prank calls to strangers: Talli thinks that's fun.
This time, a woman answers, hardly waits
for him to speak, warmth in her voice. "Oh, son!
At last you've called. At last." He hesitates,

hangs up. But something in her voice—Her number
stares up at him, somehow resonates.
He calls her back, his reticence undone.
Calling her becomes part of his day.

Until she doesn't answer. He has her
address, goes by. The house—a for-sale sign.
Neighbor says, "She died quite peacefully;

her long-lost son called every day. Some hurt
got healed." "Where is he now?"
"Oh, sweetheart, he's been dead ten years."
A ghost spoke on that line? ❖

8

SALT OF KINDNESS /
NO FAULT

SALT OF KINDNESS

No one locked up or called 911 in that town.

One night she awoke, tiptoed downstairs. The fridge was open. A teenage boy sat eating. The cauliflower! He reached over and added salt. Next, the chicken. Again, more salt.

Finally, she said, "Clean up, after…"

The youth fled. She locked up, went back to sleep.

Next morning she reached the school where she taught and perused the database. She found him alone in a classroom.

He tried to run. She held out a bag. "I brought lunch." He looked away. She continued, "With extra salt…"

They both burst out laughing.

NO FAULT

A school teacher in the quiet town,
its students know just where she lives.
One night, suddenly awake, she hears a sound—
Stands silent in the kitchen doorway, light

from the fridge—a teenage boy sits quickly
downing last night's chicken, salting every bite.
She breathes, he looks up, flees . . . Next day,
she's found his picture in the database, and finds

him in the halls. He panics, tries to flee
again. She moves and pins him with his name.
"Hunger isn't anybody's fault."

"You mean you—you're not gonna punish me?"
She sees it surfacing, his buried shame. "I brought
you lunch—" a bag, a grin— extra "with salt!" ❖

A Fool's Battle / Escape

A FOOL'S BATTLE

When his son first learned to walk, talk and read before his peers, the village headman swelled. "*My son!*" he boasted.

As the son grew, flourished, the father tightened his hold. He claimed his son merely stood on the father's shoulders.

When the village voted the son headman, the father started criticizing his son's farming methods, governance, everything. Eventually, the son stopped talking to his father.

Distressed, the father consulted a *sadhu,* a holy man. "My son forgets his duty!"

The sadhu smiled. "Look inside. What makes you grasp so tight? Life passes for all. Wise men make space for the next generation."

Escape

The headman sings the praises of his son
and yet reduces him to merely *his.*
And as the son grows up, the dad insists
that *he's* the fount, the source, the boy springs from.

And when the son's elected headman with
his own approach, the father's full of piss
and vinegar, until at last the son
won't speak to him, relationship undone.

Dad consults a sadhu, holy man.
"My son rejects me; he neglects his duty
towards me, he—" The *sadhu* stops him. "Can't

you see it, how it isn't him, it's you? He
has to live his own life. That's the beauty
of it. Sons slip from their father's hand." ❖

10

Sweet Legacies / Living Wood

SWEET LEGACIES

Summers in Delhi were unbearable. But they brought mouth-watering mangoes! One blazing afternoon my family polished off a most delectable batch. My father instructed the gardener to plant one of the seeds by the fence. Soon we moved away.

Years flew. One day, passing that street, my parents decided to visit the old house. The new residents were welcoming. My father pointed out the now fully grown mango tree he planted, to my mother. The new residents exclaimed, "Those mangoes! Another reason we love it here."

My parents laughed.

They're both gone now—having left numerous sweet mango trees behind.

LIVING WOOD

Delhi's unrelenting heat;
locals fainting in the street;
old gardener's brown and spotted hands;
sweet mango seeds left in a heap.

My father, laughing, takes one, stands.
He calls the gardener: "My good man,
please plant this seed there by the fence.
We'll see if this is mango land!"

We move. Years pass. The day came when
my father said, "Let's go and spend
an hour in that neighborhood.
Let's visit our old home again."

We went, we walked, at last we stood
outside that fence. There, living wood,
tall mango tree—right where it should have
been! Saw we'd done something—good. ❖

11

THE VOID /
HEADLONG

THE VOID

Jack's friends marveled when he jumped off a twenty-foot structure. Soon he was jumping off taller structures, gathering hundreds of followers.

"People love me," he boasted.

Soon an elbow, an ankle, then three ribs broke.

Finally, a shattered femur landed him in the hospital. Thousands of fans messaged him.

The doctor cautioned, "Stop! You'll kill yourself."

He laughed. "No. My fans love me."

One day as he jumped, his legs—crooked from injuries—caught on a ledge. Jack fell headlong. And died.

Millions chattered. Headlines screamed of Jack's daring.

For a day.

A new clown arrived—eating his way to death. Millions chattered.

HEADLONG

Jumping from a height, young John attracts
a crowd. Next time, it's higher, crowd turned fans
who start to egg him on. At last he lands
up in the hospital, bones broken, cracked.

His doctor warns him: "Keep this up, young man,
you'll soon be dead." But John just starts to laugh.
"Because I love to jump, they love me back.
I'll jump again, Doc, soon as I can stand."

The doctor, watching, has to wonder who
is jumping: John, or all his many wounds . . .
His legs so crooked now he trips and falls,

headlong. His loving fans hold him in thrall.
They lift his broken body like a prize,
while yet another fool begins his rise. ❖

12

THE RETURN /
WOMEN'S WAR

THE RETURN

Dahej: dowry

Trishna sobbed at her parents' front door, "Don't tell me to return there."

Trishna's mother glared, but let her in. Trishna, fleeing her abusive husband, wondered how long she could stay this time.

Her mother bellowed, "So much we gave in *dahej*! Shamelessly burdening us again. Wish I'd only had sons!"

Trishna's father remained mum.

Why do the "strongest" women in this society devote their energies to subjugating other women?

Soon a headache tormented Trishna. She died two days later. People asked, "Brain hemorrhage? Injury from abuse? Autopsy?"

"No need," said the mother. "She's simply returned—to where we all will."

Women's War

Trishna stands outside the house once more,
escaping from her husband yet again.
"Dowry's paid!" Mom shouts. "Go back to him!"
"Don't burden *me* with your domestic war."

"I can't go back, I can't return to him.
Look! I'm a refugee, I'm fleeing war!
I'll die before he'll touch me anymore,
before you make me live with him again."

Her dad stays silent, has to wonder why
the strongest women leave the weak undone—
this women's war . . . Trishna takes to bed,

turns to the wall; within a week, she's dead.
Abuse? Despair? "Well, we all have to die," the
mother says. "Go back where we come from." ❖

13

SAUBHAGYAWATI /
GOOD CLAY

SAUBHAGYAWATI

Panditji: Hindu priest

Saubhagyawati: fortunate woman

Panditji arrived looking harried and self-important. Trishna lay peacefully, finally. Wrapped in a white shroud. A few bright marigold flowers were strewn about. Panditji sat down and asked for Trishna's husband. Her mother replied, "He won't be coming."

Panditji barked, "Since he's living, she should be dressed like a bride." One of Trishna's sisters sobbed, "Why? He's the reason she's dead. She should go as a widow…"

An old aunt, the family's guardian of tradition, interrupted, "Quiet! Trishna was a *saubhagyawati*. Only a fortunate woman's husband outlives her. Do as pandit ji says."

Someone was sent to fetch Trishna's bridal sari.

Good Clay

Panditji's shadow in the door,
his scented feet caress the floor.
Trishna lies quite peaceful now,
bare body covered with a shroud.

"Where's her husband?" asks the priest.
"He's the reason she's deceased!"
"No matter. Dress her as a bride.
The family has to keep its pride
as long as he is still alive."

"Don't make yourselves importunate.
By dying first, she's fortunate.
A husband, he has every right
to shape her clay to his own sight.
Good clay would not put up a fight."

The priest sits back, he sips his tea,
knows nothing of her misery.
Her sister gets her bridal sari.
No one has to say, *I'm sorry.* ❖

14

Dumb Luck /
Marry And Remarry

DUMB LUCK

My parents' marriage was *so* "arranged" that they only met at their wedding!

As a know-it-all teenager, I mocked it.

They laughed. "But we're happy!"

I countered, "Just dumb luck!"

I married for love. And observed many marriages flourish or fade based on the partners' commitment—regardless of inception.

Towards the end, my mother diligently cared for my Parkinson's-afflicted father, despite her own ill-health. One day I accompanied her to my father's neurologist. He remarked on my mother's dedication, "You must've had a good marriage."

She simply nodded, smiled.

I did too—at *my* dumb luck in having landed my happily-married parents.

Marry and Remarry

My parents' marriage was so thoroughly
arranged, they first met on their wedding day!
Miss Know-it-all, I mocked them. They just played
along. "We're happy." "Dumb luck," I would say.

I left home, tasted life. Soon I could see
it wasn't just how things began. No, "we"
demands commitment on the way; we need
to marry and remarry every day . . .

My dad comes down with Parkinson's, reduced
to such a shadow of himself, days stuck
in bed or in his wheelchair, muscles useless

more and more. My mother marries and
remarries him each day. I understand
at last. Their wedding day was *my* dumb luck.

15

Samaru / Quick Learner

SAMARU

Simla: small town in the Himalayas

Samaru came to work for my newly married mother in Simla. He'd come straight from his village, unfamiliar with city ways.

One evening friends came calling. When asked to bring them water, Samaru brought out glasses to hand to them. Apologetic, my mother instructed him to bring back the water, more formally, on a tray.

Next thing, my mother saw Samaru frozen at the door, trying to balance the tray. He'd poured the glasses of water directly onto it!

Samaru's fame spread, but real notoriety arrived when he eloped with the girl-servant next door, never to be heard from again.

Quick Learner

He comes straight from his village, Samaru,
with no exposure to big city ways.
My mother hires him; she likes to play
a mentor to the young. But he's unu-

sual. When visitors come by, he waits
with empty glasses; she asks why. "Oh, you
all must be thirsty!" "Yes, but Samaru,
please bring us water; put it on a tray."

Soon he's in the doorway, can't get through,
water sloshing, spilling off the tray.
She has to laugh a little even as

she rescues him. One thing the young man has
in spades: a certain charm. Ah, yes, it's true:
he runs off with the maid next door, escapes. ❖

16

LOVE'S MUSIC /
BEGIN TO DANCE

LOVE'S MUSIC

Long ago foraging in the jungle, I heard music playing itself. The notes flew, mingling with the winds. One note stayed near, swaying, swirling about my head. As it flew, I chased it over hills, valleys, gorges. It stepped into a river. I jumped in.

The river reached the big city. The note climbed out. I followed. It played on.

Some listened, few nodded, most didn't hear it at all. Until one man stopped to dance to its music. The note rested. I touched the man. We fell in love.

It's been many lifetimes.

We're still dancing to that note.

BEGIN TO DANCE

In the singles bar, they play new songs,
music as insipid as my beer.
But one comes on and penetrates my ears—
it finds my heart: I know we now belong

together, so I follow it for years.
From town to town, from latitude to lon-
gitude, while I myself progress from pawn
to rook to queen. One day a king appears,

who, hearing it, begins to dance. Together
we escape the board, the song our guide,
our star. Insipid left so far behind . . .

Now there's days I stop and wonder whether
it's the song or us. Would we exist without it?
Or are we what made it such a hit? ❖

17

TIGHT BARGAINS / RUPEES FOR PAIN

T I G H T   B A R G A I N S

Sarpanch: the elected head of a village

Dharamraj was running for *sarpanch* in the tight village election. Daily, his buffoons shouted slogans from a jeep. One day they knocked over little Seema, breaking her leg. Seema was rushed to the hospital. Villagers chanted against Dharamraj.

Next day, Seema lay on a cot outside her home. Dharamraj arrived. At her father's signal, Seema wailed. Villagers shouted. Dharamraj offered Seema a thousand rupees. Seema wailed louder. Dharamraj doubled his offer. The wailing escalated.

Finally, at ten thousand rupees, Seema's wailing ceased.

Seema's father reclaimed the lien on his fields; Dharamraj won the election. The villagers bid the villainous jeep goodbye.

RUPEES FOR PAIN

Caught in a tight election, Dharamraj
decides to up his game so he can keep
his role as *sarpanch,* town headman. Marauding
through the village in a beat-up jeep,

his men shout slogans, praise him like a god—
brought back to earth when they hit little Seena,
break her leg. Next morning, Dharamraj
appears, offering a trade: rupees

for pain. Her father signals her to wail.
One thousand doubles, triples, turns to ten—
Only then does Seena's wailing cease.

The father pays his debts off. Alpha male,
young Dharamraj wins his election; he's
made *sarpanch* once again, rupees to spend. 

18

MANGO BONDS / MANGO DEBTS

MANGO BONDS

Summer's end. We're at the train station bidding my uncle's family goodbye. The train starts pulling out. My cousin Sunil yells to me, "I stole the mangoes!"

The next day, I write him demanding my share of the money my mom made us kids cough up for the complaining mango-seller. I never hear back from Sunil.

Next time I see Sunil is two decades later. He drives three hundred miles to help me move out, while my soon-to-be-ex-husband seethes in a corner.

As we drive out Sunil declares, "Even—on the mangoes now!"

I laugh out loud. First time in years.

MANGO DEBTS

The old train hisses, pulling out.
My cousin Sunil waves and shouts:
"I stole the mangoes! It was me!"
and then he's gone, lost in a cloud

of steam. Next day, I write him: *We*
were made to pay—us kids—so please
send me my share. I mean, you owe
me that! But we're two galaxies,

we move apart. Two decades flow
between, whole continents . . . But when I go
to leave my husband, Sunil comes
to help, said husband close to over-

whelming me. "So are we done
with mango debt?" he asks. I laugh
out loud, first time in years. I understand: the present heals the past. ❖

19

FINDING HOME / SUDDEN PAWN

F INDING H OME

At the Partition of India, 1947

Chowkidar: guard or servant

Fleeing to cross the new border, having left everything behind, they arrived after nightfall via a nonstop, two-day train.

An old *chowkidar* was waiting. He unlocked the empty house where one room had been readied for them. The widow put her youngest two down on the bed. She lay sheets down on the floor for herself and her teenage son and daughter. Exhaustion overwhelmed the heat and mosquitoes, and they fell asleep.

Next morning, they awoke to discover a summer garden with fruit-laden trees behind the house—a sight that would bring joy for years to come, despite their losses.

SUDDEN PAWN

At the Partition of India, 1947

Two days' nonstop train ride fleeing south—
the widow, her four children, refugees. In
darkness, walking through abandoned streets
to reach their refuge—one room of a house.

The old *chowkidar* turns his rusty key; she lays
her youngest on the bed, three crowd around.
Spreads sheets out on the floor, lies down
to sleep at last, despite the bugs and heat.

She dreams of all she's had to leave behind,
who was a queen, reduced to sudden pawn.
Grateful she could make her move in time,

before the border closed its hungry jaws . . .
Next morning, look, a garden, heavy hoard of fruit.
That pawn's a queen can cross the board. ❖

20

SURVIVAL OF THE CLUELESS /
A LITTLE CHAT

SURVIVAL OF THE CLUELESS

Middle of seventh grade, my best friend Saira arrived at school, sobbing, "I have cancer!" Hindi movie scenes in which the hero melodramatically dies of cancer flooded me. I started crying too.

Someone must've called our no-nonsense school nurse, Sister Pam, because soon she was upon us, "What's this racket?"

"Saira has can-cancer," I sobbed.

Undeterred, Sister Pam turned to Saira, "Who told you?"

"No one, b-but I bleed. . . in the toilet," Saira wailed.

I wailed louder.

Sister Pam slapped her forehead, "Bah! It's your period. Follow me!"

Saira and I halted our wailing, and ran agape after Sister Pam.

A Little Chat

Eighth-grade bathroom, Saira wailing;
attempts to comfort unavailing.
"I've got cancer! Soon be dead!"
Now *we're* wailing, gripped by dread.

School nurse, strict Sister Pam,
comes in to see what great calam-
ity's befallen us. "What? Cancer,
girl? How do you know?" Sobbed answer:

"Look, I'm bleeding in the toilet!
Don't tell me to just ignore it!"
Wails some more; we make a chorus.
Sister Pam, she's ready for us.

"Saira, girl, it's just your peri-
od." We stare, we stop our wearied
wailing. "Come with me," says Sister.
"We just need a little chat."
(Our mothers taught us none of that.
She did, at last. We could have kissed her.) ❖

21

The Cure /
Make A Go Of It

The Cure

An isolated, old man became ill. He was prescribed walking the streets of his town. On the first day, he came upon two poor children playing in the dirt.

He tried to stop them, "Stop playing in the dirt. You'll get sick!"

The kids ignored him. He tried again.

This time they responded, "Why?"

"So, when you eat, you have clean hands," he countered, lamely.

The kids laughed, "There's nothing to eat. We play and forget that."

Realizing his folly, the old man started helping the kids. His ills disappeared. But he never stopped walking the streets of his town.

Make A Go Of It

Isolated, old, more frail each day,
Venkat follows doctor's orders, takes
a little walk most sunny afternoon.
He sees boys playing in the dirt, assumes
a stranger's stance, strict as his father was.

"Don't play in that," he says. But they ignore
him, dirty, ragged, caught in clouds of dust.
He tries again. They stop, they stare at him.
"Why?" one asks. "Because," he says, "Because—"
how has everything become a war?—"Because
you'll need—you'll need clean hands to eat."
They laugh. "No food *to* eat! That's why we play!"

Venkat sees it, starkly: his mistake,
how karma—karma doesn't work this way.
It's *him,* been playing in the dirt, bare boned;
who's dreamed he'll make a go of it alone.
Karma—*Hey Ram!* Nothing works that way.
If he could help these boys, he'd have a home. ❖

22

LISTEN TO THEIR WORDS / HOOKED

LISTEN TO THEIR WORDS

When we reached the top of the hill, we saw an ascetic in simple robes meditating there. Curious, we approached him.

He told us he'd lived there for two years. He'd given up his materialistic life for *sanyas*, Hinduism's fourth stage of life where humans are urged to focus on detachment from the material world.

Soon, the *sanyasi* started reminiscing about the big house, three Mercedes cars and the lavish lifestyle he'd renounced. We all listened agape, impressed.

But on the way back, my mother perspicaciously remarked, "He's here but his mind and heart are still held by material things."

HOOKED

Kurti: an Indian tunic

We climb the hill, my mom and me, and at
the very top, we stop, take in the view.
And there we find a holy man, *sanyasi*,
this—renunciate. He's lived there two

whole years; me, I'm impressed. Mom asks
about his path, how he got here. "I grew
out of that shell," he says. I left the grasp
of things behind. But, oh, let me tell you—

the house I had! Mercedes cars, not one,
but two (one silver-gray, one blue). Soft *kurtas*
sewn for me from silk. Baubles on long racks . . .

We head back down. My mom says, "He's not done
with earthly things. No, they still have him trapped.
He's still a fish, caught on their shiny lure." ❖

23

LOVELY BEAUTY "SALOON" /
VANITY

LOVELY BEAUTY "SALOON"

I'd frequent *Lovely Beauty "Saloon"* (sic) whenever I visited my mother in India. For various vanity rituals—eyebrow threading, hair coloring, etc. My mother's patronage earned me special treatment.

Lovely, the owner, ran it superbly. The salon was in a shopping strip, not fancy but competent, convenient.

One day I noticed Lovely had a black left eye. Next time she told me she'd divorced her husband.

Few months later, she married Kumar, the scrawny hairstylist she employed. Six months later the shop was renamed: *Kumar's Lovely Saloon.*

Lovely was pregnant. This time her black eye was on the right side.

Vanity

I patronized it, Lovely's great "Saloon,"
indulged in rituals of vanity— hot oil
in my hair, whatever she proposed that day.
One time, a black bruise bloomed

on her left eye, and she confessed to me—
in her so lovely voice—divorce was looming:
*Lord, I'm leaving him, our marriage doomed
to violence.* Next visit, she was free

again. I get busy, months go by.
She's married Kumar, young employee.
The shop now bears his name. And I can see

she's pregnant, start to tell her my delight—
when suddenly, it's all just vanity:
this time, the black bloom rises on her right.

24

ELEMENTARY, JAMES! /
EPIPHANY

ELEMENTARY, JAMES!

Despite soaring fame for his political poetry of outrage, a malaise overtook James. Fans, drugs, therapy to excavate ghosts, nothing helped. He remembered Miss Margot, his fifth-grade teacher—the reason he became a poet. She always helped with his youthful conundrums. He decided to write to her.

His letter returned with a terse, "Passed away."

James called the school to reach her next of kin.

Weeks later a package arrived with: "My mother kept this copy of your book." James opened the book to his first angry poem.

In the margin, in Miss Margot's sensible hand was, "Clever! But. . . kindness, James?"

Epiphany

Filled with anger, outrage, righteousness,
his poems gain a modicum of fame.
With age, he spirals downward, can't quite tame
depression. Comes to see he's in a mess.

Resuscitating ghosts, there's one remains,
the woman taught him way back in fifth grade.
Made him a poet. Could her simple *yes*
release his growing *no,* take the pressure

off? Soon, he discovers she's long dead,
but someone sends a book they know she read.
It's *his*, his poems she would understand.

And in the margin, in her flowing hand,
epiphany addresses him by name:
"All very clever, yes, but—kindness, James?" ❖

FORGOTTEN LETTER /
MOVED

FORGOTTEN LETTER

The movers wrapped and packed her life in deft, raucous motions. Zohra finished making lists, something Harish would've done, if he hadn't passed. Right now, he'd be counting how, in their forty-two years, they'd tended to three kids, twice as many dogs, the garden, innumerable travelers.

Her hand passed absently over the armoire they'd fallen in love with, in Shanghai. Her fingers slid behind the door to the secret compartment.

The letter had lain there for over twenty years. Opening it, she read, *Call me. Tomorrow, the day after, a hundred years hence. I'm waiting.*

Zohra reached for her phone.

M OVED

As movers dance around her, Zohra makes
the lists Harish would do except he's died.
All those years together, how to hide
the wound? Three kids, six dogs; so many taken

in so happily. Trips to Shanghai, where this
armoire—her hand moves over weightless
wood so polished, smooth—somehow became
their own. Her hand recalls a place to hide,

forgotten twenty years, a secret drawer:
his letter tucked inside. She sits, unfolds
it, reads *Call me when you get this (old as you*

might be). Me, I'll stay hungry for your voice.
She lifts her phone— No. She's alone. His voice
has moved on, left her house and home. ❖

Slowly images recede.

They swirl and blend, here at the end.

Their colors run, their contours bleed

across the page . . . The mind can mend.

Reena Kapoor grew up all over India as an "army brat" and that wandering sensibility is reflected in her writings.

A tech executive for over twenty-five years, Reena now devotes her time to daydreaming, and writing plays, poetry and stories. Her poetry and short fiction have appeared in several literary journals and anthologies. Several of her plays have been produced by EnActe Arts in the Bay Area. Since 2011, Reena has been a Citizen Historian with the 1947 Partition Archive collecting oral histories from witnesses of India's Partition.

She graduated with an undergraduate engineering degree from The Indian Institute of Technology Delhi and a master's degree from Northwestern University.

Reena lives in Silicon Valley with her family and can be found on Substack at *Arrivals and Departures*.

THE POET

Born and reared in San Francisco, in a Victorian mansion her father liked to call Mad Manor, Kate Adams has been writing since the age of twelve, when her first short story came to her, filling page after page of a very surprised notebook. She has been writing since, mostly (as here) in sonnet forms.

In this collection, she joins forces with Reena Kapoor's stories and photographs, rendering them as poetry.

Designed  & typeset

by the authors as one in a series

of private printings of these works.

Text set in Goudy Oldstyle,

with Zapf Digbats

and Charlemagne

as display fonts.

www.ingramcontent.com/pod-product-compliance
Lightning Source LLC
Chambersburg PA
CBHW060335310726
48976CB00007B/2567